Dark Secrets

Written by Anthony Masters

Illustrated by Patricia Ludlow and Chris Brown

Contents

The Mountain Bike

1

'So what are you going to ride?' asked Alan.

'My bike,' replied Zak Bowen. 'Unless you think I should try a horse.'

'I was just wondering if it would make the ride this year.'

'No problem,' said Zak. 'My parents are buying me a mountain bike.'

The lie slipped out so easily that he was amazed. So was Alan, but for a different reason. 'I didn't think that they could aff–'

'What?'

'Nothing.'

But he knew exactly what Alan had been going to say. He was wondering if the Bowens could afford to buy their son a new mountain bike. Zak's father was disabled and his mother was a cleaner. They were on the breadline, receiving income support.

Zak Bowen and Alan Dyer had always been best friends and it hadn't mattered in the past that the Dyer family had a good deal more money than the Bowens.

The Dyers had taken Zak on holiday with them to exotic places and he was always swimming in their pool. Zak didn't feel patronised but his mother did.

'Off again with those Dyers,' she had complained, her bitterness spilling out. 'They're spoiling you rotten. I suppose your own family aren't good enough for you any more.'

Zak had reassured her, pointing out how much he loved them both and he genuinely did. But he was increasingly embarrassed that his family were so poor. At the same time, Zak was angry with himself for thinking that way.

He knew that Alan would have found him a bike for the cross-country race the following week, but he desperately wanted his own, so the lie had come automatically. The only problem was that he hadn't a clue how he was going to get it. He'd dropped himself right in it. Zak was too young to take on a newspaper round. What was he going to do?

Alan was still looking at him suspiciously so Zak lied again. 'I'm going to pick the bike up next week so I've got plenty of time to practise.'

'Bring it over,' suggested Alan.

Zak nodded, panicking to himself.

2

Time seemed to speed up, days rushing past as Zak's panic grew. Suppose he told Alan about the lie? He was bound to be sympathetic. But he didn't want Alan's sympathy. That would be the worst thing of all.

One evening after school, he went over to swim at Alan's house.

'Only a couple of days to go before you pick up that bike,' Alan said as they walked over to the pool.

'That's right,' said Zak anxiously.

'You don't sound that pleased.'

'Yes, I am.' He tried to sound more enthusiastic. 'I just want to make sure I get the right one.'

Usually a keen swimmer, today Zak just floated on his back and gazed up at the sky. When they were changing Alan asked him if he was all right.

'Sure.'

'You'd tell me if there was anything wrong, wouldn't you?'

'You bet.'

Before he left for home, Zak went to the toilet and on the way out he saw a large envelope on the Dyer's hall table. It read:

CASH GIFT FOR
ST BARNABAS CHURCH
TO BE COLLECTED BY
THE REVD SMALLBONE

The front door's wide open, Zak thought. How stupid and careless the Dyers are. Anyone could steal the envelope.

To his own total amazement, Zak folded the envelope and slid it into his pocket as he walked past the hall table and hurried out into the sunshine. 'See you tomorrow,' he yelled at Alan and leapt on to his old wreck and cycled off, trying to wave casually while the envelope seemed to bulge so large in his pocket.

3

He didn't exactly feel guilty. Instead, Zak felt an almost frenzied excitement. He deserved to have the bike. The envelope could have been stolen by anyone. If the Dyers were stupid enough to leave it out – of all places on the hall table – then they deserved to lose the money. And he deserved to have it. Zak didn't want to think about it so he closed his mind.

Zak put his rusty old wreck in the shed, feeling like a traitor. Despite the fact that he was ashamed of it, he had always loved his old bike.

He ran softly up the stairs so as not to disturb his mother in the kitchen, opened his bedroom door and flung himself down on the bed. What had he done?

Then Zak sat up and dragged out the envelope and tore it open.

He began to count the money.

The notes were in fifties and there were eight of them. Four hundred pounds. It was enough to buy the bike of his dreams. He felt a soaring feeling of joy, combined with a cold terror.

When his mother called him from downstairs he could hardly speak.

'Zak? Are you up there?'

'Yes,' he croaked.

'Why didn't you come and see me?'

'I wanted to change out of my swimming trunks.'

'Are you all right?'

'Of course I am.'

'Hurry up then. Your tea's waiting.' She sounded hurt.

Once he was in the bathroom, a sudden thought hit Zak like a thunderbolt and he staggered against the door, pushing it open. He hadn't thought this out at all. If he brought a mountain bike home, what on earth were his parents going to say?

Then the idea came to him. He would tell his parents that he had saved Alan from drowning. Maybe Alan had hit his head on the bottom after diving from a badly set spring-board.

He would go on to say that Alan had been fiddling with the board against his parents' instructions. Mr Dyer had been

very angry with Alan but incredibly grateful to Zak for rescuing his son. As a result, Mr Dyer had given him a bike. But he hadn't wanted Zak's mum or dad to thank him. Mr Dyer just didn't want anyone to know how stupid his son had been about the spring-board.

Zak checked over his lie. There were a few holes in it – but it would do. It would *have* to do.

4

After a sleepless night, Zak cycled straight over to the shop and bought the mountain bike. It was a fantastic machine, even better than he hoped it would be, with loads of gears, chunky tyres and a shiny frame.

'Want to leave the old one with us?' asked the owner. 'I've got a skip round the back for the scrap metal bloke.'

Feeling even more of a traitor, Zak rode away, trying not to think of the old wreck being taken to the skip and thrown roughly inside. Tears came into his eyes and a hollow feeling filled his chest.

Zak's parents accepted the story of how he rescued Alan much more easily than he could ever have imagined. In fact they were proud of him.

'You deserved that,' said Dad.

'I'm proud of you, Zak.' Mum was all of a dither. He was their only child and they were always looking for ways to praise him. 'But they shouldn't have allowed Alan to fiddle with that board.'

'What did you do with your old bike?' asked Dad.

'The shop are going to dump it in a skip for scrap,' said Zak.

'Well I think I'll try and retrieve it. Your cousin Richard might like to have it. It's a bit of a wreck but he hasn't got a bike.'

'Sorry, Dad. I should have thought.'

'That's all right, Zak. You've had too much on your mind.'

5

'That's a brilliant bike,' said Alan. 'Absolutely brilliant.'

'My dad saved up for it.'

'But it's not your birthday –'

'He wanted me to ride it in the cross-country race next week.' Zak paused, trying to sound casual.

Zak quickly tried to change the subject. 'What's up with your dad? He didn't even give me a wave when I came up the drive.'

'I was going to tell you,' said Alan. 'We've had a burglary.'

Zak felt sick, but he knew that he was bound to have to face it some time.

'Dad left out some money for the organ fund at the church. The vicar was meant to pick it up ten minutes later from the hall table but he was late and a thief got there first.'

'Do you know who it was?' asked Zak baldly.

'Not a clue.' Alan shivered. 'It's horrible to think a burglar came into the house.'

Zak felt sick again.

6

Next morning, Mr Dyer drove Zak and Alan to the start of the race with their bikes strapped to the roof rack. They were going to join up with some of Alan's older cousins.

'Now you've got to be careful,' began Mr Dyer as they neared the forest. He had been rather silent – strangely silent – all the way up, or so Zak thought. Did he suspect something?

The race was to be held on forest tracks which went up and down hills. The ground was muddy and Zak knew he'd have to rely on the gears on his bike.

The race started off well. Zak was feeling confident until ten minutes after the start, a sleek racing bike overtook him and came so near that he lost control.

Zak hit a tree with a devastating crash and saw a dark tunnel rushing towards him.

When he opened his eyes Zak found himself in a hospital bed.

'Welcome back to the world,' said the nurse. 'You came off your bike and you got concussion. Your parents are outside.'

When Mum and Dad came in they were quiet and uneasy.

Then Zak's secret came back to him. 'What happened to the bike?' he asked his father.

'I can probably fix it up for you,' he said doubtfully.

'You mean it's a write-off?'

'No, it will need a new front tyre and the fork is a bit bent. But you know your dad,' said Mum brightly. 'He can fix anything.'

Was she looking at him strangely? And did Dad seem distant?

'How long have I been in here?'

'You've been unconscious for a couple of hours.'

What did they know? Zak wondered.

'You're going to be all right,' said Mum. 'They want to keep you in hospital until tomorrow.'

7

That night Zak couldn't sleep. Why didn't Alan come? Zak was sure everyone knew. Maybe he had blurted his secret out when he had been unconscious. Were they all waiting until he had recovered to contact the police? Was he too young to be arrested? In the end he panicked and called the nurse.

'I've done something terrible,' he told her.

'What is it, Zak?' she asked sympathetically.

When he had finished, he said, 'So that's why Alan and his parents haven't been to see me. They know I'm the thief.'

'I don't think that's the reason,' the nurse told him gently. 'Mr Dyer phoned to see how you were. Alan's grandfather's been injured in a car accident and they're all down at another hospital. It never rains but it pours.'

With a cold feeling seeping around his heart, Zak realised he need never have confessed to the nurse at all.

'What should I do?' he asked.

The nurse looked back at him steadily. 'Tell your friend.' She got up. 'Now, you're to get some sleep. OK?'

Zak did exactly as she told him. He felt at peace.

8

When he woke, however, he found himself looking up at Mrs Dyer. Standing behind her was Alan. Immediately, Zak tried to sit up, desperately afraid.

'I took the money,' he whispered, his heart beating so fast he could hardly breathe. 'I lied and I –'

Mrs Dyer took his hand in a cool grip. 'I know,' she said. 'We both know, don't we, Alan? And we also understand why it happened.'

'Have you told the police?'

'Of course not. My husband's replaced the money for the church and we suggest you work it off. I know some people who need some gardening jobs done. It'll take a long time to pay it all back, but I think you'd want to, wouldn't you, Zak?' She smiled down at him.

'I could sell the bike, and I've got some pocket money that I've saved. I promise I'll pay back all the rest.' Zak hesitated before adding, 'Do my parents know?'

'We offered to replace the bike and they said we mustn't be so generous again. That's how we all found out what had happened. Your mum and dad are upset of course, but I know you are too.'

Zak looked at Alan. 'I s'pose you

don't want to be mates any longer –'

'Of course I do. But it was a silly thing you did.'

Zak knew he was right.

Zak lied about getting a new bike. What were the consequences of his first lie?

Thin Ice

1

Gary and Terry knew they shouldn't go on the ice. There was even a warning sign, pointing out how dangerous the frozen lake was:

BEWARE
THIN ICE
DO NOT SKATE.

'Bet you're too chicken,' said Gary. He often made up dares because he wanted to prove how tough he was. 'I went on it last night,' he lied. 'All by myself.'

'It's dangerous,' said Terry. He was in the school football team and Gary had just been dropped, which was another reason for the dare.

'Don't be a wimp,' replied Gary.

'You go on then,' dared Terry.

'I told you I –'

'Go on again then. Prove yourself.'

Terry and Gary gazed at each other aggressively, almost as if they were about to have a fight. Neither could back down. Not now.

'OK.'

Gary stepped on to the black and glittering ice, looking to see if anyone was around, but that winter's afternoon, the park was deserted. It was just before four and already getting dark. Gary shivered. A cutting little wind had got up and he could see frost forming on the trees and bushes.

He slid cautiously a couple of metres away from the bank. The ice seemed solid enough.

'Look, it's safe,' he shouted.

Slowly Terry joined him and soon they were sliding about, yelling with excitement.

Then Terry began to move away from the shore towards the centre of the lake.

Gary wanted to shout at him to stop, but he couldn't. After all he had told Terry the ice was safe.

Suddenly he was terrified.

Terry waved at him impatiently. 'Come on out here.'

Gary slid slowly towards him, feeling the fear inside.

Then he heard the most dreadful grinding sound and to his horror he saw Terry disappear through a hole in the ice in the middle of the lake.

Without thinking, Gary began to slide towards the place where his friend had just been.

Although the crack had spread, the ice seemed firm right up to the hole that had so horrifyingly opened up. Dark water slopped about inside.

'Terry,' he yelled. But there was no sign of him at all.

Then, to his horror, Gary saw a shadow under the ice.

'Swim the other way,' he bellowed. 'The hole's over there.'

But he knew Terry couldn't hear him – or see him either. He was trapped.

Panic swept over Gary. He had to get him out, but how? The black ice seemed to wink up at him mockingly and the wind ruffled his hair with freezing fingers. He wanted to call for help, to let someone else take over, but there was no one. Terry's going to drown, he told himself – and it's all my fault.

Through the waves of panic, Gary still knew that somehow he had to break the surface of the ice so that he could release Terry. He pulled off one of his heavy boots, saw the shadow again, knelt down quickly on the ice and began to attack its surface.

Gary had completely forgotten about any danger to himself. He had to get Terry out now; he knew he only had seconds.

At first the ice was too hard to break. Below him he could see Terry's shadow, imagining his face gazing up in desperate appeal.

Then the surface splintered and cracked, and water lapped at the edge of the black ice. Was Terry alive?

Suddenly he saw his friend's fingers reaching for the edge of the ice and he gave a great shout of joy.

Grabbing his wrists, praying the ice wouldn't break up again, Gary slowly began to haul Terry out of what might have been his watery grave.

Gary put his arm around Terry's waist and helped him back to the shore. He was terrified that any minute he would hear the deadly cracking sound again and they would both go under.

Terry was making a wheezing sound and his whole body seemed to be shaking. At last they reached the bank and he sat down, shivering violently.

Gary took off his coat and wrapped it around Terry. Slowly, Terry warmed up enough to speak.

'I thought I was going to drown,' he gasped.

'You'd better come home with me. Have a hot shower. I can lend you some dry clothes.'

But Terry wasn't listening. 'You saved my life,' he said.

Gary shook his head. 'We were idiots and it was my fault. I dared you to go on.'

'And I dared you to go into the middle. You *still* saved my life.' He was still staring up at Gary with a gratitude Gary was sure he didn't deserve.

'Let's go back to my place,' suggested Gary.

'What about your parents? They'll be furious.'

'They're out – and they won't be back till seven.'

'If anyone finds out we've been here on the ice we'll be in big trouble,' said Terry fearfully. His shivering was easing a little now, but Gary knew he had to get him warmed up fast.

'We'll keep it secret, won't we?'

Terry nodded shakily.

2

They made their way quickly across the park to Gary's home, Terry's sodden shoes slopping and slipping on the hard frosty grass.

When they arrived home, he went straight into the shower while Gary searched for some clothes that his mum wouldn't miss. Luckily both he and Terry were about the same size.

But when Terry came out still shivering Gary became really worried.

'I feel hot *and* cold.'

'Maybe you should get checked up by a doctor – or the hospital,' Gary forced the words out. He didn't want them to get into trouble but he didn't want Terry to be ill either.

'If I do, it'll all come out and we'll be in for it,' replied Terry.

They stared at each other uneasily, and Gary remembered that he had been in quite a bit of trouble at home already. Deliberately ignoring the warning notices and going on the ice would mean that Dad would stop him going out for months.

'I'll run home,' said Terry. 'That'll make me feel better. I can get up to my room without them seeing me.' He gave the most gigantic shiver.

'What about being late?'

'If they see me I'll say I've been with you. They won't mind.'

Gary watched Terry run out into the darkness. Was that him coughing? he wondered. It was a horrible rasping sound. But he knew they both had to keep the secret – somehow.

3

Gary slept badly that night, tossing and turning, worrying about Terry. He kept remembering the shivering – and that awful, racking cough. But when he woke up he felt much more optimistic. Terry was tough. Terry was in the school football team. Terry was going to be all right – for sure.

When Dad came in from his early morning run, Gary got a terrible shock.

'They're dragging the lake in the park,' he said. 'Crowd of people down there, but they haven't found anyone yet. There's a great crack in the ice and a big hole, as if someone was fool enough to skate on it and then fall through.'

Mum went rigid. 'How awful. Do you think they were local kids?'

'Well if they were local, they should know better. That warning sign has been up for a fortnight now,' said Dad.

'You'd never go on that ice, would you, Gary?' Mum was so anxious that he felt he'd been kicked in the stomach.

'Of course I wouldn't.'

4

Gary felt both afraid and incredibly guilty as he ran across the park. He knew it was far more his fault than Terry's – after all, he had dared Terry in the first place.

When he arrived at the lake he saw the crowd of people, two police Range Rovers and a diver, slowly walking away from the ice. Then Gary spotted a boy he knew from school.

'They found anyone, Jack?' he asked anxiously, noticing the crowd was beginning to break up.

'They called the search off. The police say there's no one in there.' Jack looked almost disappointed.

5

Where was Terry? He wasn't in class. Could he be late? Gary gazed round the room, his anxiety beginning all over again.

'Where's Terry, Mrs Magee?' he asked.

Mrs Magee, his teacher, smiled at him. She had been worried about Gary for some time. He was such an anxious boy. Now he looked even more so. 'Terry's ill today, Gary.'

'What's wrong?'

'Some kind of 'flu, I think. Now we must get on. I want you to get out your –'

But Gary didn't hear what she was saying. All he could think about was Terry's awful shaking and his horrible rasping cough.

6

'You heard?'

'Heard what?' Gary looked up suspiciously at Trevor Simms. Trevor was a real stirrer. He loved to find out people's weak spots and then wind them up.

'About your mate, Terry.'

'Yes?' Suddenly Gary started sweating.

'He's in hospital.'

'Don't be stupid.' Gary's first reaction was anger rather than fear.

'He is,' grinned Trevor.

'How do you know?'

'I saw his sister at break.'

The anger disappeared and it felt as if ice was creeping into Gary's throat. He thought he was going to choke. 'What's the matter with Terry?'

'He's got pneumonia. Couldn't have anything to do with the park, could it?' Trevor asked sneeringly.

Gary searched Trevor's malicious eyes. 'I don't know what you mean. You're talking rubbish, as usual.'

'So why did my grandad see you walking out of the park last night with Terry, all soaked and shivering?'

'Oh that.' Gary's mind raced but he couldn't find an explanation. Panic overtook him.

'Yes, that,' said Trevor who didn't want to drop the subject.

Then Gary had an inspiration.

'We were playing football and Terry fell over in the long, wet grass.'

'My grandad didn't mention football.'

Gary shrugged. 'It was getting dark. Maybe he couldn't see the ball?'

Trevor scowled. 'Sure he didn't fall into the big, wet lake?' He chortled and then began to chant, 'Who's got a secret? Who's got a secret?'

'Shut up – or I'll make you!' yelled Gary and immediately everyone in the playground looked their way.

'You two going to have a fight?' asked Jack, hurrying across in delight.

But Trevor backed off. He revelled in stirring but he didn't like life getting physical.

7

Gary didn't know what to do. Suppose Terry died? Could he be dying now? He had to get to him somehow. Had he told his parents about falling in the lake? Gary prayed he hadn't. But suppose the doctors needed to know what had happened? Suppose they couldn't treat him if they *didn't* know? Gary began to sweat even harder and his heart began to thump painfully.

'Is there something wrong, Gary?' asked Mrs Magee as she crossed the playground. 'Do you want to have a talk?'

'No,' he snapped at her rudely, and then tried to repair the damage. 'No, thank you. I'm fine.'

'Are you sure?'

He nodded miserably.

'Well –' She began to move on. 'You know where to find me if you change your mind.'

Somehow Gary got through the day, desperate about Terry, but at the same time equally concerned he might have confessed their secret.

On Gary's way back across the park, he met Trevor, who came up to him, gazing back at the now deserted lakeside and grinning unpleasantly.

'Going for a slide on the ice, are you? Going to get another ducking?'

Before he could stop himself, Gary ran up to Trevor and punched him hard in the chest. He fell back with a whimper and a howl.

Gary knew where he was going now. He'd made up his mind. He was going to the hospital to see Terry.

8

When he got off the bus at the General Hospital, Gary went straight to reception and asked where Terry Hutchings was. The woman gazed at him doubtfully before telling Gary he was on Esher Ward.

'How is he?' he stuttered.

'You'll have to ask Sister. Aren't your parents –'

But he had already gone.

As soon as he arrived on Terry's ward, Gary went straight up to the Sister. He had no fears for himself any more. They had vanished. All he wanted was to find out whether Terry was dead or alive.

'Terry Hutchings?' he asked.

'Terry's been moved to a private room,' the Sister replied. 'I think his parents are on their way up. Are you a relative?'

Gary almost gasped with relief. Then he began to wonder how bad Terry was. 'I'm his brother. I ran up the stairs in front of my parents.' He was amazed that the lie had slipped out so easily and confidently.

'Be nice and quiet then. He's first on the right, down the corridor.'

Knowing he had hardly any time at all, Gary pushed open Terry's door. He was lying in bed with a tube going into his arm and there seemed to be an awful lot of dials and switches around. A TV set was flickering in a corner.

Terry looked pale but he grinned when he saw Gary.

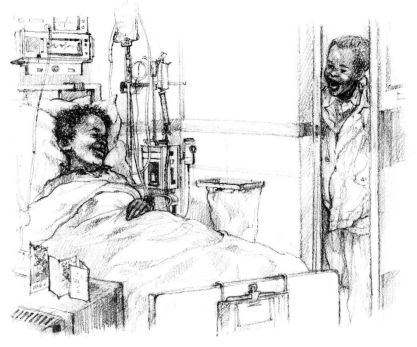

'How did *you* get in?'

'I said I was your brother.'

Terry laughed and then began to cough.

'Your parents are on their way up so I haven't got long. How are you?'

'I'm OK. The doctor said I was getting better and, by the way, I didn't tell anyone.'

'What *did* you tell them?'

'I just said I'd been feeling lousy for a couple of days but I didn't want to own up to being ill in case I lost my place in the football team.' He began to cough again.

'Thanks,' said Gary. A sense of release filled him.

'So I've done the right thing.'

'I haven't,' Gary replied shamefully. He knew he couldn't hang on to the secret any longer. He started to walk towards the door.

'Where are you going?'

'Don't worry. I'll be back to see you soon.'

Gary hurried out and began to run

down the corridor. Then he saw Terry's parents slowly walking towards him.

He realised that if he didn't confess now, he never would. He had lied so easily – and all those easy lies had been completely believed. If he didn't own up immediately he would go on lying for ever. And if that happened, he would no longer be the person he thought he was.

'Hello, Gary,' said Mrs Hutchings in surprise. 'Where did you spring from?'

'There's something I have to tell you,' said Gary. 'Something that's completely my fault.'

What persuaded Gary to tell the Hutchings 'the truth'?

Should Gary have told his parents about the accident straight away?

Hide and Seek

1

'We never eat cake.' Mrs Jackson was tall and good looking and she obviously wanted to get rid of the Bryants as soon as she could. 'But thank you for the thought.'

Mrs Bryant nodded and turned back down the Jacksons' garden path. Her face was red and her lips were working, but no sound came out.

Mrs Bryant closed the front door of her own house, put the cake down on the kitchen table and looked up at Tracy and Sam. 'They don't eat cake.' She was amazed.

'I think she is incredibly rude,' snapped Tracy, furious that her mother should have been rejected. 'You go to all that trouble to make our new neighbours a cake and she treats you like that!'

'What does it matter?' said Sam, who was much more laid back. 'We can eat the cake.'

'That's not the point, you idiot.' Tracy
stroked her mother's arm.

'I wonder what the Jackson kids are
like,' said Sam thoughtfully.

Sam put on his rollerblades. As he
came out of the house, he saw a boy and
girl kicking a ball to each other in the
Jacksons' front garden.

'Hi!' said Sam.

They were twins with short fair hair.

'I'm your next door neighbour,' he
said. 'You've just moved in, haven't you?'

The boy nodded reluctantly but the
girl turned her back on Sam and began
to move towards the house.

'What are your names then?' he asked. 'I'm Sam.'

The boy turned and followed his sister to the front door. She slammed it behind them.

'They're weird,' said Sam at tea.

'Maybe they're just shy,' replied his father. 'Want to keep themselves to themselves.'

'They were rude to Mum,' said Tracy.

'They were rude to me!' Sam began to explain what had happened but his mother interrupted.

'I think we should stop crowding them. Leave them alone to settle in.'

'I'll leave them alone all right,' said Sam who was hot-tempered. 'I don't want to be friends if they don't.'

Next morning, the Bryants saw Mr Jackson pushing a large Ford van out of his drive. Unlike his wife and children, he was short and puny looking.

'It won't start,' said Dad. 'We should go and help.'

The whole family rose eagerly to

their feet.

'Let me give you a hand.' Bob Bryant owned a garage in the nearby town. He was also big and brawny. 'If you get in and steer, I'll give you a push. Do you know what's wrong?'

'Battery,' said Mr Jackson. 'Or plugs,' he added a little more doubtfully.

'Would you like me to have a look? I'm a mechanic.'

'No thanks. If you can give me a push down the hill I'll be away. I can get the car fixed in town.'

'Hop in then.'

Mr Jackson didn't smile or even bother to thank them. Instead he got in rather reluctantly and took the wheel.

'Ready?' yelled Bob Bryant and they all began to push.

Eventually the aged Ford started with a nasty black cloud of exhaust fumes that enveloped the Bryants, making them splutter and choke. Then Mr Jackson drove away.

'He didn't even wave,' said Tracy, her anger returning.

2

'That's odd,' said Sam. It was a Saturday and he was up early. He was going to play in his usual football league, but it was an away match. Tracy was looking forward to going ice skating.

It was a grey winter's morning and the light was poor.

'What's odd?' asked Tracy.

'That VW's been parked opposite the Jacksons' house for half an hour now.'

Tracy came to the window and squinted into the murky February light.

'It's got a couple of people sitting in it,' she said. 'As if they're watching the house. Weird, isn't it?'

As Sam and Tracy watched from the window, they heard the sound of an engine and saw the car driving slowly away, turning right at the crossroads and disappearing from view.

Mrs Bryant was closing the curtains on the bleak wintry afternoon. 'The Jacksons never seem to come out,' she said.

'They're a funny lot, all right,' muttered Bob Bryant. 'They certainly keep themselves to themselves.'

Later that afternoon, Sam and Tracy went out for a ride on their bikes.

'Look.' Tracy grabbed her brother's arm. 'They're back.'

The couple were sitting in the same VW. The man was reading a newspaper and the woman was behind the wheel, staring ahead.

Tracy looked back up the road and saw a small Renault with what looked like a single figure behind the wheel. He, too, seemed to have the Jackson home under surveillance.

'What's going on?' demanded Tracy.

Then the VW suddenly started up and began to drive back to the crossroads. After a minute or so the Renault did the same.

'I don't get it,' said Sam.

'I don't like it,' replied Tracy.

3

'Two cars watching the house. That's dodgy.' Mr Bryant went to the phone.

'What are you going to do?' asked Mum. 'Ring the Jacksons?'

'I'm going to call the police.'

'You can't do that.'

'Just watch me. They could be terrorists – or assassins. I mean, we could be in the middle of a shoot-out, couldn't we? We're entitled to protection.' He dialled, waited and then began to explain.

Eventually he was halted mid-sentence, there was a long pause and then he started to explain all over again. This time he was allowed to finish. Then he had to listen. After a while he thanked the person he had been talking to and put the phone down, looking satisfied.

'Well?' Tracy, like Sam and his mother, could hardly bear any more tension.

'The police aren't watching the

house, but they're going to check on the road from time to time and –'

'From time to time?' interrupted Sam. 'That's no good. They'll never catch them like that –'

'Catch who?' asked Mum. 'I think we're all jumping to conclusions.'

Tracy and Sam looked at each other. They weren't so sure.

'They might be burglars – waiting to break in,' Tracy suggested.

'No chance,' said Dad. 'They wouldn't make themselves so obvious.'

And that seemed to be that.

4

Sam went on his bike again the next morning but Tracy, who had a cold, didn't join him. This time he rode down the side street that went round the back of the Jacksons' house, down to the bottom of the road and turned right towards the common.

Then he came to an abrupt halt as he saw a young girl running in the opposite direction, her cheeks streaked with tears, glancing back all the time as if she were being pursued. Sam suddenly recognised her as one of the Jackson twins.

'Hey,' he said as he crossed the road. 'Something wrong?'

She slowed down and stared at him in renewed fear and then he saw a flicker of recognition.

'It's only me – Sam Bryant. What's happened?'

The tears were flooding down her cheeks and she was shaking. 'This man –'

'What did he do?'

'He scared me.'

'What did he *do*?' repeated Sam gently. 'You've got to tell me.'

'He was in a car.'

'Did he ask you to get inside?'

She shook her head. 'He was watching me.'

'Where from?'

'Down there. By the common.' She was more under control now but Sam could still feel her fear.

'Where is he now?'

'He drove away.'

'What's your name?'

'Sandra. Sandra Jackson.'

'Do you want to walk home with me?'

She looked grateful, but still seemed uneasy as they hurried down the road.

'Do you go to school round here?' he asked.

Again she shook her head.

'Are you going to?'

'I don't know.'

Silence enveloped them.

'I'll speak to your dad then. Tell him what happened,' Sam said as they approached the Jacksons' gate.

'No. It's all right. I'll tell him.'

'Your dad needs to ring the police. That man could be dangerous.'

'Don't worry.' Her voice trembled. 'He'll do it.' She paused by the gate. 'Look, thanks – I'm really grateful. I'm sorry if we haven't seemed that friendly.' She stopped abruptly, as if she had said too much. Then she hurried towards the front door.

When he got back in the house, Sam told his father what had happened to Sandra Jackson.

Immediately, Mr Bryant went to the phone and spoke to the police again. When he came off the line this time, however, he seemed puzzled.

'All they can say is that they'll look into it.'

'What else can they do?' Mum yelled, having overheard from the kitchen.

Now she mentioned it, they weren't quite sure.

5

Tracy had always been a light sleeper, and that night she was wakened by a noise from outside. Getting out of bed, she ran to the window and, pulling the curtain aside, peered out into the foggy night. There was a car outside the Jackson house – a different one this time. Tracy thought it was a Fiat.

Then her attention was caught by someone running away down the front path and jumping into the passenger seat. The car drew away slowly at first and then began to pick up speed towards the crossroads.

For a few seconds there was an almost deafening silence, and Tracy found herself waiting expectantly for something to happen.

Then it did.

There was a loud, dull explosion and a sheet of flame shot out from inside the Jacksons' front door.

Tracy didn't take long waking up her parents and brother, and in only a matter of minutes she and her parents were outside, heading for the Jacksons' front garden, while Sam called the rescue services.

Smoke was pouring out of the door and they could also hear the crackling of flames.

They could see Mr and Mrs Jackson opening their bedroom window. Sandra and her brother were doing the same.

Mr Bryant dashed back to get a ladder but Sandra didn't wait. She began to crawl over the ledge, her eyes wide with panic.

'Don't jump!' yelled Tracy. 'My dad's gone for a ladder.'

Then Sam came racing up the path. 'They're on their way!' Suddenly he saw Sandra on the window ledge. 'Stop, don't move!' he shouted.

'Sandra,' yelled her brother. 'You've got to wait.' He tried to make a grab at her but missed as she toppled over the edge.

6

Tracy and Sam ran to break Sandra's fall but they missed her and she fell on to the grass with a cry of pain and one leg twisted underneath her.

Meanwhile, Mr Bryant had arrived with the ladder and had propped it up against the wall, underneath the twins' bedroom window. As he began to climb up it, Mrs Jackson called down, 'What's happened to my Sandra? What's the matter with her?' Mrs Jackson hadn't realised that Sandra had jumped out of the window.

She was lying on the ground and groaning. Tracy shouted up, 'I think she's broken her leg.'

Mrs Jackson called out something else but her voice was drowned by the sound of a siren.

As the firemen hosed down the hallway of the house, the three Jacksons were hurried away to a police car and Sandra was lifted into an ambulance.

The police car was still stationary and they saw Mrs Jackson speak to her husband and then to one of the policemen. Hurriedly, she got out again and walked quickly back to the Bryants.

'I want to explain,' she said. 'But I haven't got much time. My husband is a key witness in a very important criminal trial and we've all been moved from safe house to safe house. This was our latest,' she said, looking very worried. 'I can't thank you enough for all you've tried to do for us and I'm sorry we seemed so stand-offish but I hope you'll understand we had to be. When this is all over, we'd like to thank you properly.'

'There's no need –' began Mrs Bryant.

'There is. There's every need.'

'The couple in the VW –' began Tracy.

'They were plainclothes police – and so was the young man in the Renault. But I'm afraid the gang got at us during a change of shift.' Mrs Jackson almost broke down, but one of the policemen came and hurried her away. In seconds the car was speeding up the road.

A crowd was gathering as the other residents woke and came to watch the fire that was now under control. Huge snakes of hoses surrounded Sam and Tracy as they listened to the buzz of radios from the fire engines and police cars.

The Bryants walked slowly back to their house. As they went, Sam said, 'It must be awful for them – always having to hide. Never being able to trust anyone.'

'Maybe it'll stop soon. Do you think they *will* contact us?' asked Tracy.

Sam shrugged.

Smoke hung like a heavy cloud over the estate and Tracy shivered. Something had come into their lives that was cold and hostile and threatening – something she had never really known or felt before. She wondered how long the Jacksons would have to keep their secret.

In what ways were the Jacksons unusual neighbours, and why?

Grace

1

'Let's have it then.'

Grace loomed over Jo, tall and gangling. There was something hard about her eyes. They were large, commanding, and there was hatred in them.

They were standing in the bike sheds which were at some distance from the school buildings. Jo had gone to collect some homework which she had left in her saddlebag and Grace must have followed her.

'Come on. Hand it over then.'

Jo wasn't going to hand over her lunch money to anyone; even Grace who was much stronger than she was.

'No,' Jo said forcefully.

Grace stepped closer, her fists tightening. 'You want to get hurt? You will if you don't hand over your lunch money.'

Jo was small and attractive, and although she had only just arrived at her new school she had settled in well. Jo had already made lots of friends and she was popular. Grace was not.

'I'm not giving you anything,' said Jo quietly. 'Now please go away.'

'I'm not going anywhere.'

Grace came even closer and grabbed Jo's arm, twisting it up behind her back. The pain was awful. 'Little Goody Two Shoes. Teacher's pet. Crawler.' The words were harsh and Grace's voice was bitter and angry.

'Let me go,' yelled Jo, but Grace clapped a hand over her mouth and wrenched her arm higher. The pain was now unbearable. She would do anything to make it stop – anything.

'Hand it over!' demanded Grace.

'All right,' sobbed Jo. 'Just let go, that's all.'

Grace waited a couple of seconds before loosening her grip. 'Hand it over then.'

Jo gave Grace her lunch money and Grace walked away without even a backward glance.

Jo was cross with herself. She should have stood up to Grace. Grace shouldn't be allowed to get away with it. She dried her tears and went back to class after morning break.

At lunch time Jo told her best friend Helen, 'I feel a bit sick. I don't want any lunch.'

Helen was concerned. 'Shouldn't you go to the office?'

'No. I'll be OK. I just feel a bit dizzy. I'll go for a walk round the field.'

'What's that bruise on your arm?'

'I fell off my bike on the way to school.'

'I really think you should go to the office and –'

'No!' Jo almost ran away from her friend. 'Leave me alone. I'm all right.'

2

'Hand it over then.'

Jo whipped round. This time Grace was looking in Jo's school bag. Grace's big eyes were full of anger. She had picked her time. There was no one else around because the bell had just gone, and for once Jo had been late getting to her classroom. She had felt so ravenously hungry all yesterday afternoon that she had eaten a huge tea and gone to bed with a blinding headache.

This morning she was exhausted and already her teacher had told her to wake up and pay more attention.

'I've got to eat.' Jo's voice shook. 'I'll be ill if I don't eat. I felt terrible yesterday.'

'Hand it over,' said Grace.

'You can't hurt me here. I'll scream, and one of the teachers will come. You'll be in real trouble then.'

Grace gave Jo a thin-lipped smile. 'My mates will get you after school.'

'What mates?' asked Jo. She was
pretty sure that Grace didn't have any.

'They're at my old school. They'll do
what I say. They'll beat you up.'

Jo hesitated.

'They'll get you on the way home,'
Grace snarled.

There was no knowing how
powerful, how evil, Grace might be. Did
she have these mates? Jo gazed into her
eyes and saw the menace.

Humbly, without saying any more,
she handed over her lunch money.

3

'What's going on?' demanded Helen as they walked towards the canteen.

'Nothing.'

'You were late into class – so was Grace. Is she getting at you?'

'Of course not,' denied Jo.

'Was she with you?'

'No.'

'Then how come you were both late?'

'I don't know. I'm not coming into lunch. I don't feel well –' Jo was on the edge of tears now.

'Oh yes, you are,' snapped Helen. 'I'll give you some lunch money.'

'I've got my own.'

'I don't think so.' Helen sighed. 'I don't think you've got any, not now. Can't we talk about Grace?'

'There's nothing to say,' said Jo.

4

'How did you pay for your lunch then?'

Jo gasped and felt a hollow feeling in her stomach. How did Grace manage to catch her unawares, always on her own?

It was a dismal rainy afternoon and Jo was walking home alone. She was determined to stand up for herself this time.

'Helen only bought me some crisps.' Grace fell into step with her, as if they were friends. 'Must be nice to have a mate,' she said.

'I thought you had loads, like those girls from your old school.'

'Oh, I do.' Grace immediately pulled herself together.

They walked on in silence.

'How about stopping being teacher's pet then?' There was an even harder edge to Grace's voice now.

'I don't know what you mean.'

'Yes, you do. When we were late into class, you didn't get into trouble, did you? It was only me, as usual.'

'It was *your* fault I was late,' protested Jo.

'Mr Browning didn't know that, did he? You always have your hand up in class – showing off all the time.'

'You're ridiculous,' said Jo, increasing her stride.

'Am I?' Suddenly Grace grabbed her arm, pushed her into an alley and up against the high brick wall. Jo howled with pain. 'Stop being a goody-goody in class, right?'

The pain seemed much worse than last time.

'Got it?' Grace was almost shouting.

'I've got it.'

Grudgingly Grace released her. 'And if you don't – I'll get you – just me. I'm not going to bother with my mates.'

Because you haven't got any, thought Jo – at this school or any other.

5

Grace's eyes had been on her all morning, and although Jo tried to work hard, she made the simplest mistakes. It was Grace who kept putting her off.

By the afternoon the class teacher, Mr Browning, was getting worried. He called Jo over to him and spoke quietly to her.

'What's wrong?' he said gently. He and Jo got on well.

'Nothing.'

'Come on, Jo. What is it?'

'I'm just a bit tired, that's all.'

'Any reason?'

'I haven't been sleeping well.'

'Why's that?'

'I don't know.'

Mr Browning sighed.

'I'm sorry.' Jo was near to tears.

'Nothing to be sorry about. You need to talk to someone, Jo,' said Mr Browning, sympathetically. 'I hope it'll be me – and soon. Now go and sit down.'

'To that friend of yours? Telling her how you're getting bullied?'

'I haven't said a thing.'

'You'd better not. Now you can get me some sweets.'

'I haven't got any money.'

'That doesn't matter. Just go in that shop and nick them for me. I'll have a couple of Mars bars.'

Jo felt her life was now completely out of control. 'That's stealing.'

'You got it in one.'

'I'm not doing it.'

'I'll get you – really hurt you this time. You don't know how far I can twist that arm back.'

Suddenly Jo knew she would have to go into the shop and steal. Grace was all-powerful. She could really hurt her.

Jo hurried into the shop, leaving Grace outside, watching her.

She glanced at some magazines and then at some comics. The shop was crowded and the owner was busy serving behind the counter with his wife. The sweet section was just behind the magazines, but Jo knew that to grab the Mars bars and walk out would be far too much of a give away. If only she could buy something.

Then Jo remembered that she hadn't spent all the extra lunch money that Helen had given her. There was 15p left. She could buy some liquorice chews while pocketing the Mars bars at the same time.

Slowly, over-casually, Jo picked up the liquorice chews and then tried to slip the Mars bars into her pocket. One of them fell out.

The owner of the shop was suddenly standing in front of her, his face full of indignation. 'Just *what* do you think you're doing?'

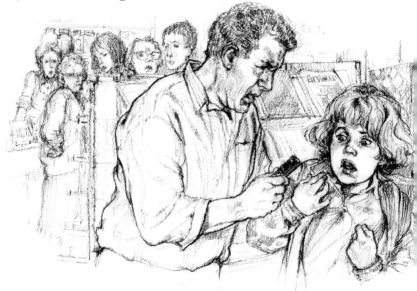

'Buying some sweets.' Jo felt hot all over, knowing she was blushing, her throat so dry and tight that she could hardly get the words out.

'By putting them in your pocket? I don't think so. You'd better stay where you are, young lady, while I call the police.'

'Please,' Jo half whispered. 'Don't do that.'

'We *always* prosecute shop lifters,' he said as he went to the phone.

Through the shop window Jo saw Grace riding away. She must have detected trouble.

7

'Why?' asked her astounded mother. 'Why did you steal them? Is something the matter? You've never done *anything* like that before.'

'I don't know.'

'You don't *know*?' Jo's mother felt halfway between rage and despair.

The policewoman had brought Jo home in an unmarked car, lecturing her all the way. Jo had felt humiliated. They wouldn't take it any further this time, the policewoman had said. But if it ever happened again –

'I just don't *know* why I did it, Mum.' Jo was utterly horrified at what she had been forced into doing. She would never forget what had happened. But she knew she couldn't tell her parents about Grace. If she did, Grace would know and Grace would go on hurting her.

Her parents were disappointed in her but they still loved her.

That night she slept fitfully, wondering why Grace was being so horrible. Why did she like hurting people?

Towards dawn Jo awoke with a sudden and unexpected thought. Who loved Grace? Did anyone? Even at home? Certainly no one did at school. Was *that* the problem?

At half past six, Jo got up and went down to her parents' bedroom and knocked on the door.

'Yes, love?' yawned Dad.

That was the word – the best word in her life – love.

'Mum asked me if there was anything the matter –'

'That's right, dear,' said her mother, kissing her on the forehead.

Jo began to tell her parents about Grace.

8

The headteacher saw Jo first and then she sent for Grace. Later she asked to see Jo again.

Soon it all leaked out, even though Jo had said nothing to her friends.

Grace openly denied anything had happened at all. Perhaps she's bullied other girls, thought Jo, and they've been too frightened to say anything to anyone. As a result, the class kept close to Jo, almost acting like bodyguards until she felt she couldn't breathe. They did the opposite to Grace, not speaking to her at all.

A few days later, Jo was taking her bike out of the shed. By chance it was the first time she had been alone since everyone had stopped speaking to Grace.

Then a shadow seemed to fall across the sun, and then on her.

'What do you want?' All her fears returned as Jo gazed into Grace's big eyes.

But there was something missing. She couldn't see the hardness, the hatred any more. Instead, Grace's eyes were misty with tears.

'What's the matter?' asked Jo uneasily.

'No one will speak to me.'

Grace had her hand up.

'Yes?'

'It's after half past three, Mr Browning. I don't think the school bell's working.'

Mr Browning glanced down at his watch. 'It's not time yet. Bring me your work so I can see how you're getting on.'

'But I didn't understand the question.'

'You never do, Grace.'

6

This time, Jo walked part of the way home with Helen who continued to try and find out what was going on. But she didn't get anywhere.

Eventually Helen left her, still worried and no nearer to finding out what the problem was.

When Jo turned the corner, Grace suddenly appeared on her bike with a squeal of brakes. It seemed as if she had come from nowhere.

'You been talking about me?' Grace looked hard at Jo.

'No.'